ADVENTURE PARK

MONSTER MAYHEM

By Cavan Scott • Illustrated by Abby Ryder

Titles in the Adventure Park set

Dinosaur Danger

Monster Mayhem

Pirate Peril

Candy Crisis

Cosmic Chaos

Rainforest Riot

Medieval Madness

Pyramid Panic

Badger Publishing Limited,
Oldmedow Road, Hardwick Industrial Estate,
King's Lynn PE30 4JJ

Telephone: 01438 791037
www.badgerlearning.co.uk

2 4 6 8 10 9 7 5 3 1

Monster Mayhem ISBN 978-1-78464-335-5

Text © Cavan Scott 2016
Complete work © Badger Publishing Limited 2016

Publisher: Susan Ross
Senior Editor: Danny Pearson
Editorial Coordinator: Claire Morgan
Illustration: Abby Ryder
Designer: Bigtop Design

Contents

Meet Emily. Her grandfather owns Adventure Park. It's the best theme park in the world!

Meet Jacob. He's Emily's best friend.

Meet Frank. He's Emily's pet hamster.

Together, they test Adventure Park's new rides.

Some of the rides are magical. Some of the rides are scary. Some of the rides are dangerous. But ALL of the rides are exciting!

Join Emily, Jacob and Frank on the adventure of a lifetime.

Cast of Characters

Emily

Jacob

Frank

Vocabulary

winced – shrank in pain or fear.

dazzling – really bright.

glinted – shone with reflected light.

looming – standing over someone.

vegetarian – a person who doesn't eat meat.

locomotive – the engine that pulls a train.

CHAPTER 1 Ghosts and Monsters

The ghost train carriage rattled along the rails. Usually Jacob found these things funny, but not this time. This time the ghosts and the monsters that were chasing them were real!

Emily looked over her shoulder as the vampire and the werewolf raced after them. Both had sharp fangs and blood-red eyes. Bats flocked around the monsters as ghosts filled the air.

"Stop them!" shouted the vampire.

In front of the carriage, Frank ran ahead in his hamster ball. "I knew this was a b-b-bad idea!" he squeaked. "What are we going to do?"

For once, Emily was out of ideas. She had never been so scared!

But wait! We've jumped to the middle of
our story!

Just why are Emily, Jacob and Frank on the run
from monsters?

Well, it all started when Albert Sparkle-Trousers
bounced up on a pogo stick.

Albert was Emily's grandfather and the owner of
Adventure Park.

He also had no idea how to control a pogo stick.

With a CRUNCH, the old man landed on Jacob's
left foot.

"Ow!" winced Jacob.

"Sorry!" said Albert and then landed on Jacob's right foot.

"Stop it!" moaned Jacob.

Albert jumped off the pogo stick. "I'm just so worried about all the ghosts and monsters!"

"All the what?" asked Frank, Emily's pet hamster.

"There are ghosts and monsters all over Adventure Park," Albert explained. "It's been happening ever since I opened my new ghost train!"

Jacob rubbed his sore toes. "And let me guess," he said, "you want us to check it out?"

"I would go myself," Albert said, "but I need to wash my, er, eyebrows!"

Frank shut himself in his exercise ball. "I want to s-s-stay here," he squeaked. "I'm s-s-scared of g-g-ghosts!"

Emily picked up the ball. "Don't be silly. I'm sure there's nothing to be afraid of."

Emily wasn't so sure when she saw the ghost train ride. It was found in the scariest corner of Adventure Park. Twisted trees lined the streets and there were gravestones everywhere. Even in the toilets!

"W-w-why does it have to be so spooky?" Frank whimpered.

"That's why people come here," Jacob said. "To scare themselves!" He sounded nervous himself.

"The sooner we ride the ghost train, the sooner we can get out of here," Emily said.

She led them over to a creepy little carriage that sat on rusty tracks. They climbed in and the carriage starting rolling forwards.

Clackity-Clackity-Clack

Clackity-Clackity-Clack.

"Where is it t-t-taking us?" moaned Frank.
He was shaking inside his ball.

"The tracks go past that creepy old house," Jacob
said, pointing towards a crumbling building.

The carriage passed beneath the shadow of the
house. Emily felt the hairs stand up on the back
of her neck.

Emily breathed a sigh of relief. "See?" she said as
they continued on their way. "There's nothing to
worry—"

Before she could finish her sentence, the doors
to the house crashed open. A vampire and a
werewolf raced out onto the tracks and began
chasing after them.

"Get them noooooooow!" the werewolf howled!

CHAPTER 3 The Chase!

Frank jumped so hard that his ball leapt out of Emily's hands. It landed just in front of their carriage.

"Help!" the hamster screamed, running ahead. "M-m-monsters!"

Emily looked over her shoulder. The vampire and the werewolf were right behind them. Their fangs glinted in the moonlight and their claws slashed through the air.

Even worse, the monsters had been joined by fluttering bats and wailing ghosts.

She turned back to Jacob. "Can't you make this thing go faster?" she asked.

Jacob shook his head. "There are no controls. It's driving itself!"

The monsters drew closer and closer.

"Stop!" the vampire shouted.

"No way, blood-sucker!" Emily yelled back.

The werewolf let out a roar of frustration and jumped forwards. It landed on the back of the carriage and snarled at the children.

It was going to attack them!

Then, a dazzling light swept over the werewolf. The monster looked up in terror as something big rushed towards them.

"Nooooooooooo!" the werewolf howled. "Don't eat me!"

WHOOMPH!

One minute the werewolf was on the back of the little carriage and the next it was gone.

Whatever had grabbed it whizzed behind them, moving fast.

And then it was gone, but not before it crashed into the back of the carriage. The children were thrown into the air and landed with a bump.

Frank ran over to them in his ball.

"Are you OK?" the hamster asked.

Emily couldn't answer. She was too scared to speak. The vampire was looming over them!

"P-p-please don't bite us!" Frank squeaked.

The vampire looked confused for a moment and then burst into tears.

"OK, I wasn't expecting that!" Jacob said.

"Waaaaaah!" wailed the vampire. "Brian used to love biting! It was his favourite hobby!"

"Brian?" Emily asked.

"Brian the werewolf," the vampire sniffed. "He was my best friend and now the Ghost Train has eaten him!"

The vampire started to cry again. Behind him, the bats and the ghosts joined in!

Emily looked at the overturned carriage in confusion. It didn't look like it could eat anything, let alone a werewolf.

"What do you mean?" she asked.

The vampire shook his head. "Not that one," he said, pointing a long, bony finger. "Look!"

Emily turned and saw what had knocked them off the tracks.

It looked like an old steam train, but had a terrifying head where an engine should have been. Its eyes were glowing and its huge mouth was full of teeth.

"Wow," Emily said. "It's a real ghost train. The spirit of an old locomotive!"

The vampire nodded. "And it's been scaring us silly. It eats monsters for tea!"

"So, that's why people have been seeing ghosts and monsters all over Adventure Park," said Jacob. "You've been hiding from the train!"

The vampire nodded. "That's why we were chasing you. Brian thought you might be able to help!"

"You weren't trying to eat us, or drink our blood?" asked Jacob.

The vampire pulled a face. "Don't be disgusting. I'm a vegetarian!"

"That gives me an idea," said Emily.

"It does?" said the vampire. "What are you going to do?"

"We're going to catch a ghost," Emily told him.

"And how are we going to do that?" Frank asked.

Emily looked at Jacob. "We just need some bait!"

"Why does it have to be me?" asked Jacob. He was dressed in an old white sheet with holes cut out for eyes.

"Because Frank is too small," Emily said, making sure that Jacob could see. "And I can run faster than you!"

"That doesn't make sense," Jacob said. "If you can run faster, you should definitely be the one dressed up as a ghost!"

"Trust me!" Emily said and put her fingers in her mouth to whistle.

"Hey Ghost Train!" she shouted. "Come and get another spooky snack. One tasty ghost ready to gobble up!"

Jacob swallowed. "I've changed my mind," he said. "I don't want to do this any more!"

"Too late," Frank squeaked. "Here it comes!"

The Ghost Train thundered towards them, smoke belching from its funnel.

Jacob screamed and started running. With a cry, he tripped on the sheet and fell over.

"Help!" he shouted.

"I can't look!" wailed the vampire.

"CHOO CHOO!" bellowed the Ghost Train.

It swallowed Jacob with one gulp!

"Jacob!" Frank squealed. "It's eaten him up!"

"Just watch," said Emily with a sly smile.

The Ghost Train frowned.

The Ghost Train groaned.

The Ghost Train gave a burp.

And then...

"YUCK!"

The Ghost Train spat Jacob out of its mouth. That wasn't all. Brian the werewolf and all the other monsters came shooting out too.

"That was disgusting!" the Train moaned and raced away, its wheels clattering.

"It's gone!" Frank cheered, as Brian the werewolf and his vampire friend hugged.

Emily grinned. "The Train eats ghosts and monsters. I guessed that it would hate the taste of a human," she said. "Just like a vegetarian vampire hates the taste of blood! I doubt we'll see the Ghost Train again!"

Beside her, Jacob pulled off his sheet. He was covered in spooky, sticky slime.

"I suppose I should be grateful it couldn't stomach me," he groaned.

"That's the spirit," laughed Emily.

Questions

1. **Whose feet did Albert bounce on?** (*page 8*)

2. **Why couldn't Albert go with the children?** (*page 10*)

3. **Who was scared of ghosts?** (*page 10*)

4. **What was the werewolf's name?** (*page 20*)

5. **What had been eating all the ghosts and monsters?** (*page 21*)

6. **What disguise did Jacob wear?** (*page 23*)

Meet the Author

Cavan Scott spends his days making up stuff – and he loves it! He's written for *Star Wars*, *Doctor Who*, *Adventure Time*, *Skylanders*, *Angry Birds*, *Penguins of Madagascar* and *The Beano*! He lives in Bristol with his wife, daughters and an inflatable Dalek called Desmond!

Meet the Illustrator

Abby Ryder is a cartoonist who loves comic books and video games. Her greatest life ambition is to one day become best friends with a giant robot.